KU-375-633

Salford power

AXIS education

Acknowledgements

Cover design: Oliver Heath, Rafters Design

Brinsford books are a direct result of the findings of a two-year authoring/research project with young offenders at HMYOI Brinsford, near Wolverhampton. Grateful thanks go to all the young people who participated so enthusiastically in the project and to Judy Jackson and Brian Eccleshall of Dudley College of Technology.

First published in Great Britain by Axis Education Ltd

ISBN 1-84618-000-7

Axis Education PO Box 459
Shrewsbury SY4 4WZ

Email: enquiries@axiseducation.co.uk

www.axiseducation.co.uk

Chapter One

"What's happening, Matt?" John asked.

I shrugged my shoulders. "Can't be assed with school."

"Come on. We'll go to Scottie's and see what he's doing."

We used to see him whenever we didn't want to go to school. Scottie never went to school. Even when he did go he was usually sent back.

We turned the corner into Scottie's street. The unmarked police Astra was parked a few yards ahead.

"No way! The police are at Scottie's again!"

"We'll just chill here till they've gone," said John.

Just as we were about to sit down, two familiar faces walked out of the house. They got into the Astra and drove past us. We smiled and stuck two fingers up at them.

"Yeah, that PC Tudor's a right dick, innit? The daft pig took my cigs off me the other day, saying it was because I'm only thirteen," I grumbled.

We walked up to Scottie's. His brother answered the door.

"What's happened to your Jordan?"

"Got nicked for theft of a laptop," his brother explained.

"Tell him to come over to John's when he gets back, then."

We walked back across the estate. "Got any money to throw in for a weed?" asked John.

"Nah. I ain't got enough."

"Come on. We'll go for a graft."

We came on to Mocha Parade car park and saw a BT van parked up.

"Shall we do that?" I asked.

"Yeah, but wait till them guys get off."

I grinned. I might have only been 13 but I did know how to break into a van.

We waited for the two men to walk on to the parade. When they went we ran over and kicked off the back panel of the van. In the back there were loads of cables and screws and things like that. At the end of the van we saw the laptop bag and the Bosch hammer drill case. We grabbed them and ran off towards the estate. When we were safe we opened the laptop bag and pulled it out.

"Fucking hell!" John said.

"What?"

"It's a shitty IBM ThinkPad."

"How much will we get for that?"

"About £50 and £30 for the drill."

It was easy to sell them because we knew where to go. After we'd got rid of them we went round to our mate Stan's and sent him for a weed.

When he came back John started toasting two cigs for a mix.

"Youse been grafting?" Stan asked.

"We got a Bosch hammer drill and an IBM ThinkPad from Mocha."

How much did you get for them?"

"Fucking £60!" John spat.

"It takes the piss that, dunnit?" I moaned.

Chapter Two

That was sort of how we got started. Then time went by and we got into nicking cars. We'd nicked them before, but only when the older boys had left them on the field. As we got older, we decided to nick them for ourselves.

About eight o'clock one night we were all sitting up at the mazies, bored and getting pissed.

"What should we do?" asked Scottie.

"Shall we go for a car?"

Only four of us decided to go for a car because all the rest wanted to stay with the girls. John, Scottie, Andy and I went to my Auntie's to get a screwdriver to nick the cars with.

I pressed the buzzer on the intercom as the others shuffled about the car park, pretending to play footie.

"Hello?" said a familiar voice.

"It's me, Auntie Lynne."

The lock buzzed and the door opened.

"What do you want this time?" she asked.

"Have you got a screwdriver, please?"

"Where's that one I gave you last week?"

"I got chased in a car and lost it."

She shook her head but she laughed. She's safe like that, my Aunt. She knows she can't stop me so she goes with the flow. She found me a screwdriver – a Stanley 5 mm.

"See you later!" I shouted up the stairs.

"Be careful!" she yelled back.

I met back with the others and we jibbed across the estate towards the outskirts of town. We used to get all our cars from there. It was full of car parks. When we got to the first of them there was a really great Cavalier, just waiting for us to take. The guard was at the other end of the car park so John and Scottie sneaked over.

I saw them looking in the windows checking for an alarm or immobiliser. A few seconds later John had the screwdriver out tanning the door. After a while I heard the dead locks click up and the door opened. John had always been good at nicking cars.

When they got in the car I heard the panelling being ripped off. After that he capped it and the car started. Scottie called me and Andy over. When we got there we had to snap it with them. John sat in the passenger seat with his foot in the steering wheel and Scottie was in the driver's seat with both arms wrapped round the steering wheel. Andy and I got on 1,2,3 snap. We heard the pins drop. John checked to see it was done properly because we didn't want the steering lock to come on while we were driving.

We were all buzzing. This was the best car we'd ever had. None of us had said a word while we were nicking the car, but when we had it away and off the car park we all started laughing.

John was driving. "It's rapid, this," he said.

"Wait till all them see it," I said.

"Fuck 'em. They're not getting in. They couldn't be assed to come for a car. They can do it."

We drove out of the outskirts and came to a set of lights. By this time we had the radio on full blast. It was some shit but none of us was bothered. We were just buzzing with the car. When the lights went on green John said, "Watch this!"

He put his foot down. The car took off. I could hear the engine roaring. We smoked it home back to the estate. "Yeah, that's a bad car!" everyone shouted. Before the Cavalier we only used to get shitty cars like Escorts and Fiestas.

"Put on a show, John," Andy said.

We got back into the car and headed towards the top of the street, handbrake up. John grabbed the steering wheel and swung the car back round facing everyone again. He spun it off. The wheels were screeching. We could hear everyone shouting but none of us could make out what they were saying because the music was up.

Then suddenly, "Dibble!" Andy hollered.

"Where?" John spun his head round.

We all looked through the back window. The unmarked VR6 was shooting towards our back end. John slammed it into first and we heard the gears crunch. He put his foot down and we took off. By now the VR was right behind us. Lights flashing. Siren blaring.

We took a quick left down Lower Broughton Road, straight up towards the lights. We sped through the lights at about 75 mph. The VR6 slowed down behind us.

"See ya later!" shouted John.

We came to the top of Lower Broughton Road. We could see the VR6 in the distance, and it was gaining on us.

"Go left here!" I shouted to John.

He flung the car round the corner. Tyres were screeching and sticking to the floor.

At the next bend two police transits were lying in wait, trying to block the road off.

"Over the hedging!" John shouted.

We bounced up the kerb and went round the back of one of the police vans. The VR6 was right behind us once again.

"We're gonna have to bail this soon or there'll be bare police out," I said.

"We'll bail it on the gravel, then," answered John.

We carried on driving. Behind us a police Mondeo 24V had joined the VR6 and two transits in the chase.

We dodged through the estate and ended up back on Lower Broughton Road round Mocha bend.

"Shit!" screamed John.

The car slid all over the road, up a hedge, and slammed into a tree. We were all bailing out as the police came round the bend.

Chapter Three

A strong smell of sweat hit me as the officer opened the cell door. The door shut behind me. I looked around. There was a bench at the end of the room with a blue mattress on it and there were stains all over the walls. I needed a piss.

At the toilet I was nearly sick. The bottom of the pan was blocked up with toilet roll and shit.

I was feeling gutted about getting nicked. Everyone does the first time and I knew this wouldn't be the last time.

It felt as if I'd been in there for days when finally the cell door opened. It was the same cop that had nicked me.

"Come on, your Nana's here," he said.

My heart dropped. She's gonna kill me, I thought.

At the front desk I could see my Nana waiting. From the way she was looking at me I knew I was dead.

"Wait till you get home," she said. "Your Grandad's not happy."

I got a caution. I didn't care a fuck about that. I was just sad for upsetting my Nana.

We got home at about 1 am and my Grandad had gone to bed. Nana had been silent all the way home but once we got inside she sighed. "What am I going to do with you?"

"It wasn't my fault," I said.

"It never is, is it?"

"Oh, shut up, moaning all the time."

"You'll shut up in the morning when your Grandad sees you."

When I went downstairs in the morning, ready to go to school, my Grandad was waiting. I could see it was not going to be good news.

"Think you're clever?" he asked. "Why did you do it?"

"Do what?"

I should have known that would make my Grandad see red. "You know what," he stormed.

I shrugged. "I wasn't gonna stand there while everybody else did it, was I?"

"I tell you this, do it again and we're finished!"

When my Grandad had taken the dog for a walk I asked my Nana how she knew I had been nicked. "John came and told me," she said.

Oh, well. She'd have had to know sometime. And I wouldn't have got out so quickly if she hadn't come for me.

On my way to school I met up with John and went on to Scottie's as usual.

"What happened to you last night, then?" he said with a grin.

"I only got a caution."

"I thought I was going to get nicked as well. The pigs nearly snapped my arms."

On the way over to Scottie's we saw Stan and Andy.

"We're going for a graft. Coming?"

Silly question. John and I went with them. We mooched about all morning and didn't get one single graft, but when we got back to the estate, Scottie and the others had an Aprilla 125 Vision that they'd taken from the Dolby Hotel car park.

It was twenty past three. Scottie dropped me off at mine. I told him I'd meet them on the estate later. When I got in my Nana said, "Been to school?"

"Yes, why?"

Slap, right across the face. Boy, did it sting!

"What the fuck are you doing?" I shouted.

"Liar, you didn't go to school because I saw you with John and the other two!"

It was time I took control of my own life. "So fucking what?" I told her coolly. "I'm not going to school again."

Then I ran upstairs, got changed and opened my drawer. I took a tenner and some gloves and went out.

"Don't expect me back later," I said at the front door.

Chapter Four

After I'd turned 15 we started to nick better and faster cars. Nana and Grandad had come round and supported me every time I got nicked. Well – they knew they couldn't stop me. I was grown up now.

So everything was good. Well, almost everything. The older boys were getting on our cases for always joyriding. We knew about doing rams because that's what the older boys did.

We'd just got the 325i from town and were putting it in the garage when Scottie's phone rang.

"That was Will," he told me. "Told him we had a 5i and he said do we want to go on a graft tonight."

After tea I told my Nana I might be late because I was doing something.

"Have you got your key?" was all she said.

While I was having my tea John had phoned Scottie back and told him we were doing Oscar's in town. And that we had to meet them at 9 o'clock, down on their estate in Ordsall.

I phoned Scottie at half eight to check he'd got the scanner from his gaff before we met up.

As we stood on the estate a car turned off Lower Broughton Road. It started bolting towards us and we knew straight away it was John and the others. They pulled up. It was a Prelude-Vtec.

"It's fat, that," I said admiringly. "Where did you get it from?"

"Harry Ramsden's car park."

They waited for us while we got the BMW from the garage and checked we had our balis, gloves, and scanner – and the duvet cover to put the clothes in. The garage stank of petrol.

Andy and I got in the back with some bricks we had ready to throw at the police if we got chased. John and Scottie got in the front. When we reversed out, Andy said, "Where's the wrench?"

"Fuck!" Scottie jumped out and ran back into the garage to get it. Finally we pulled round the corner and flashed our lights to tell the others, parked behind another car, that we were ready.

On the way into town we pulled up at a set of lights and a police Omega pulled up facing us. We could see the Prelude edging forward, ready to take off with us behind them. All our hearts nearly stopped. But when the lights changed to green the Omega turned right and went a different way.

"I thought we were on a hotters, then," said John.

"I know," I laughed.

We got into town and pulled up outside Oscar's. "Balis down," Scottie said.

We all pulled our balaclavas down and jumped out of the car. John and the others already had half the shutter up when we got on it with them. It just flew up and the alarm was screaming by this time. People that were walking past were looking at a bunch of masked youths running in and out of the shop. Did they do anything? Did they hell!

Inside the shop it was dark, but we could still make out where the clothes were. Andy had hold of the duvet cover, while Scottie and I were getting racks full of jumpers to put in it.

Scottie then found the coat rack and was starting to clean that out. It was chaos inside the shop. Everyone was running about into each other. It was funny in a way.

We had the duvet cover nearly full, when we heard car horns blasting. We dragged the cover outside, and John and his lot had thrown their goods into their car. We opened the boot of the BM but the duvet wouldn't fit in, so we had to empty some of the clothes in the back with us.

"Hurry up, they're coming over."

We jumped into the BM. We could hear engines revving, both ours and theirs. As the Prelude passed us they beeped to let us know they were going their own way home.

All in all, it only took a few minutes to do the job and be on our way, but it felt as if we had been there for ages. On the way back we were all shouting and laughing, our adrenalin still going.

We got home without seeing any police. After we'd put the clothes in the gaff of a bird that we knew, we put the BM back in the garage so that we could use it again to go out and get another car.

In the morning Nana started on me, before I'd even finished talking to Scottie on the phone. "What time did you get in?"

"Not late, and I'm going out now," I shouted. I know my Nana brought me up and that, so I do owe her something. But, like I said, it was time I took control of my own life.

There was a car on the drive of the gaff where we'd put the clothes the night before. I saw Scottie coming out of the house.

"Who's that?"

"The guy I said was coming when you phoned," he told me.

"How much have you said for it all?"

"Three thou, six hundred."

"What's that each?"

"Nine ton."

In the end the guy gave us three and a half grand for it all. When we'd counted the money and split it four ways we gave £50 to the bird whose gaff it was for letting us keep the stuff there. Then we all went into town to spend some of our dough.

I was buzzing. It was the first time I'd had proper money for myself. I had new clothes and three ton in my drawer.

Chapter Five

Beer Trading is a little club in town where everyone goes on a Friday night. The best thing is you don't have to wear jeans or shirts. So I just threw on my Nike hooded top, some Nike pants and the black TNs that I'd bought that day. I got two ton out of my drawer and phoned a taxi. Scottie was ready to go when the taxi called for him.

"Where are we meeting them?" I asked.

"In there."

"Say we don't get in?" We were both underage and without IDs.

"We will."

The taxi dropped us off just around the corner from the club. When we got to the door it was lucky for us that one of the older lads was standing there talking to the bouncer.

"Easy Matt, Scottie," he said.

We didn't even have to pay to get in. I thought to myself, I could get used to this. The inside was different, compared to what I thought it would look like. The bar was at the far end and the dance floor was in the middle with tables and chairs around it. There were already loads of people in there. We had already seen the older boys all sitting at the back of the club. We went over and shook hands.

One of them said, "You did Oscar's the other night, didn't you?"

"Mad-heads!" said another.

I went to the bar to get Scottie a drink and had to shout to the barman so he could hear me, the music was so loud. They were playing old-skool so I didn't mind. On the way back from the bar I saw Scottie chatting to two birds.

"Here's your drink." I passed it to him and walked back to the older boys. A few minutes later Scottie came over.

"That bird over there said, 'Is there any chance?'"

"What, for a disco dance?" I said, laughing.

"I'd just been getting into her mate when you came over with my drink. She said, 'Who's that?' so I told her your name. And she said, 'Go sort it out for me.'"

"Safe. I'll do her and you kill her mate off."

Just as I said that one of the older boys shouted me over. "Do you want some of this?"

"What is it?" He seemed to be playing with a tenner note.

"Ching."

"What the fuck's ching?"

"Coke, you mad-head."

He rolled a note up and passed it to me.

"What do I do with it?"

"Put the end of the note in your nose, and sniff that line up."

I did what he said. Put the note up my nose and sniffed. After I'd done that my eyes started watering a bit and I got a mad feeling at the back of my throat. I kept having to sniff up.

"Go tell Scottie there's a line here for him."

I went over to Scottie. "You're wanted over there."

"What for?"

"You'll see," I said with a grin on my face.

"You talk to that bird that wants to go with you then."

"Hurry up, then." I can't believe I said that.

The girl Scottie had been talking to came over. "Are you Matt? You going to sort it with my mate?"

"Why? Are you sorting it with Scottie?" My heart was beating.

"Yeah."

"Tell her to come here, then."

By this time Scottie had come back and I could see him sniffing up. I just started laughing.

"Where are those birds gone?"

"I told them I'd kill them both. Nah – I didn't. They'll be back in a sec."

And just as I said that, the two birds came walking over. The one that Scottie was getting into pulled him off across the dance floor. I was left with the bird that wanted to get into me. I thought, 'Shit – what am I going to say to her?' Lucky I was pissed and coked up or else I wouldn't have said anything to her.

Her name was Lisa, and she came from Little Hulton. When I told her I was from Lower Broughton she said, "My cousin lives down there."

"Yeah? What's he called?"

"Tom Summers."

I burst out laughing and said, "No offence, but the guy's a dirty crack-head."

"What's so funny?" she said.

Wrong. Better get on with my next tactic. "Nowt," I said. "Want a drink?"

She asked for Brandy and Coke.

"Are you going to get randy on the brandy?" I said, smiling.

There wasn't a lot of time for that. The club closed ten minutes later. It was three in the morning and cold outside. Lisa was with me and fuck knows where Scottie was. I saw the older boys and said, "What are you up to now?"

"We're going back to some gaff for a party. You coming?"

"I can't. I'm with some bird."

"Look at you! First night out and taking birds home!"

I walked over to Lisa and said, "What you going to do now?"

"I don't know. I was supposed to stay at Hannah's, but she's gone with your mate."

"Do you want to stay at my gaff?"

"Yes, if you want."

"I want you to. Do you?"

"Yes."

I thought she looked a bit cold because her nipples were sticking out through her top. I took off my own top and gave it to her. She said, "Thanks", and gave me a kiss.

We managed to get a taxi after only about ten minutes. At home I put my key in the front door and opened it. I looked back and said, "What are you stood there for? Come in."

"Is that you?" Nana shouted sleepily. "Put the alarm on when you come up."

"Right."

We sneaked into my room and I took my T-shirt and pants off and got into bed. She took off her top and skirt and got in next to me.

"Fucking hell, you're cold," I said.

"Well, warm me up, then."

Chapter Six

Two more years went by. I had gone from petty thief to full-time criminal. And there'd been lots of girls on the way. I loved the money, the clubs, the respect it brought with it. But there was one thing that was inevitable – jail.

I was now seventeen and had gone past the point where probation or community service was a possibility. I knew before I went up to the dock from the cells that I'd be going to jail that day. The Group 4 guard put the cuffs on me outside my cell and said, "Come on, you're up."

When I came up the stairs into the dock I looked behind me, and I saw Nana and my bird Katie.

"I love you," she said. I couldn't say anything. I just smiled.

After the judge had finished his speech about how what I had done was bad, the words came that I had been dreading.

"For the offence of burglary and causing injury while taking a vehicle without the owner's consent, I sentence you to 18 months ..."

I felt my heart skip a beat. My solicitor had told me to expect around 6 months. This was my first time in jail but luckily for me I was going to Hindley. I knew plenty of people in there, so I knew I'd be alright.

The sweat box came to a stop at the front gates of the prison. Well, this would be my home for the next nine months at least. The Group 4 guy came and opened the door and took out his cuffs. I had to put my right arm out while he cuffed it. As I walked off the bus it hit me.

I'd been sent to jail. I was gutted.

Chapter Seven

After I'd been down to reception, got my number and changed into prison clothes they took me to F wing. When I got there they were on Assoc – the time when you could do stuff like play pool or make phone calls. This was nothing like I thought jail would be. On my way up the stairs to my pad I had seen about six people I knew so I felt at ease already.

About two months down my sentence, John came in. He'd been nicked for agg-twoc, dangerous driving and all the rest that comes with the parcel. I was buzzing when I saw him.

"What wing are you on?"

"F wing."

"Yeah, man! Same as me!"

Later on that day I blagged the screw on our landing to pad me and John up because we said that we were cousins.

After John got out I only had a month left and I'd learned a lot in prison. But the thing that kept coming to mind was the word Securicor. I'd heard the amount of money you could get out of them was unreal. When I was released I decided that I was going to do Securicor vans.

When I walked out of the gates Katie was there waiting for me. She'd stood by me a lot while I was in jail. I'd only been with her about a month and a half before I was sentenced and she'd waited for me. I was grateful for that.

And I loved her. The worst thing I could have done. Fall in love. I never thought I'd see the day. But I did. And it changed my whole outlook on life.

Now I had a reason to make big money because I wasn't earning for myself any more. It was for both of us.

Chapter Eight

We'd been watching a drop off for a few weeks now and we were about to hit it. The Securicor van always came on Wednesday, at 10.15 am The guy got out, went to the back of the van, got a box and went into the Cash and Carry. Exactly six minutes later he came out.

We planned to run behind the guy and go straight into the manager's office to get the lot while the time-lock on the safe would be off. We knew the layout inside. Getting to the manager's office wouldn't be a problem. The main problem was the amount of people in there. The simple way would be to run in with a gun, but the older boys told us never to use a gun. It just makes it worse if you get caught. So we came to the conclusion that we should run in with machetes.

Now we had all that sorted, we needed a car. That night we went out for one. We were just cutting through an estate in Prestwich when Scottie nodded.

"Check that. There's a T-4."

Scottie turned our car round and pulled up at the side of the drive where the T-4 was parked. We got out of the car, put our balis on and crept round the back of the house. The back door was a joke. All we did was put pressure on it and it flew open. Scottie got the Maglite out of his pocket and shone the beam. We sneaked around looking for the keys. They were hanging up in a cupboard on the stairs. We went back out to the car and looked up at the bedroom window to make sure no one was about.

We opened the car door, let the handbrake off and pushed it round the corner to where John was parked, waiting for us.

"No way! Youse have got it!" John exclaimed.

"You know the one!" I answered, smiling.

We started the T-4 up and Scottie told John to follow us. It even had a full tank of petrol. We parked it in the lock-up and decided to change the plates the next day.

Katie had said she'd be waiting up for me. I glanced up at the clock. It was five to four in the morning. "She's gonna kill me," I thought. I crept into the room. She was fast asleep. "So much for waiting up for me," I said to her as I moved her over.

I put my arms round her and gave her a kiss. Then I fell asleep. I woke up and Katie was wide awake next to me.

"What time did you get in?"

"Not late," I lied.

"Where was you?"

"I had to do something."

"What?"

"What do you want to know for?"

"'Cos you're my boyfriend."

"So what's that got to do with it?"

"Forget it!"

"Right. You mentioned it. So don't get moody when I tell you."

What she didn't know she couldn't tell anyone.

John found another T-4 and noted down its number for us to use the registration. He was back in an hour or two and we put new plates on the one we had nicked. We celebrated by going to Maxime's, a club in Wigan. We knew two of the bouncers and they just nodded to let us past. We walked over to the back of the club. That's where everyone from Salford stands. All the older boys were in there that night so we went and stood near them.

I came home at ten to three in the morning. Everyone else went to some slag's house for a party. I couldn't be assed, and my bird was at home so I just went there instead.

Wednesday came and I was up at eight in the morning because we had to be ready for ten. We needed to be there before the Securicor van was. We met up and parked on a pub car park opposite the Cash and Carry and waited.

The Securicor van pulled up at 10.15. Right on time. John started the T-4. We left it for a minute to give the guy time to go in and open the safe.

"Right. Now!" yelled Scottie.

We put our balis down and got the machetes ready. John pulled up near enough outside the Cash and Carry doors. We jumped out and ran in. There weren't as many people as we thought there'd be.

"Fucking stay where you are!" I screamed at the two women on the cash tills. Andy and Scottie stayed in the front part while I ran through two doors towards the manager's office. The door was locked when I got there. I took a few steps back and flew at it. It blew straight off its hinges. I ran in and the Securicor guy was there, taking the cash out of the safe and putting it in a box.

"Put the fucking money in the bag, dickhead!" I threw him the bag. The manager began to get up from his chair, but I yelled at him, "Lie on the floor!"

The guard began filling the bag with plenty of notes. I felt like jumping in the air with joy. When he finished filling the bag up I stared at him hard. "Stay where you are!"

I went back down the corridor and threw open the double doors.

"Come on!" I shouted at Andy and Scottie. We ran outside and jumped in the T-4. John smoked it all the way home. We abandoned the car and got off on foot towards Scottie's gaff, ready to count the money.

There was just over eight thousand each. I was buzzing. It was the most money I'd ever had. I didn't know what to spend it on.

After that job we started doing them all the time. We were making more money than I could have dreamed about. I was buying clothes and going out all the time. I gave my Nana and Grandad a few grand. I bought a brand new Golf V6-4 Motion out of the showroom.

I was finally living the life I'd always wanted.

Chapter Nine

We sneaked up the drive and looked through the windows of the house. There were two men sitting in the living room.

"Shall we just kick the door off or come back later?" I asked Scottie.

"Fuck it, we're here now. We'll take the door off."

We both counted to three and ran at the door. BANG! It flew open. We ran in. The men's faces went white.

"Where's the fucking car keys, prick?" I shouted.

"I don't know what you mean," one answered shakily.

As he finished speaking Scottie punched him in the face and started wasting him.

"I'll ask again. Where's the fucking keys?"

"Here, here," said his mate, fumbling in his pockets for them. We grabbed the keys and ran outside to the Subaru.

The next morning we found a double-up for the Subaru and wrote the reg down to have plates made. We'd clocked a fat graft and wanted to use the car for that.

In the early hours of the next morning we got to the garage and took out the Subaru. "What time is it?" I asked.

"Twenty past three," Scottie replied.

"Shit! We'd better hurry up."

We got to Salford Precinct in about fifteen minutes and parked the Subaru in a street facing it. It felt like hours, hiding in the bushes facing the TSB bank, but I knew it would be worth the wait. I'd been carrying a grid and my hands were sore. It was heavy, so I felt confident it would do the job.

"Matt – here." John passed me half a cig.

"Safe." I finished smoking it, put the dimp in the dirt and covered it up. Just as I did that the Securicor van pulled up outside the bank.

"Get in the Subz, John," Scottie whispered. We waited for the guard in the van to get out and open the bank doors.

We gave him five minutes. John went to drive round. We ran across the road. Got to the bank doors and threw the grid at the glass doors. They just shattered right away. We ran in and saw the guard trying to shut the back of the cash machines he was filling up. I ran over and whacked him across the helmet with a wrench.

"Get the fuck back!" Scottie shouted to the other guard.

We both started filling the two bags. We emptied the cash machines and started getting the piles of note in the open boxes on the floor into the bags. Scottie spun round and saw the guard on his mobile.

"What the fuck do you think you're doing?" He booted the phone out of the guard's hand. Scottie picked up a computer monitor and threw it at the guard. We heard John beep the horn.

We looked at each other, ran outside and jumped into the Subaru. We were pinned to our seat as John floored it.

We got back to the garage, put the Subaru in and ripped the plates off. Then we ran over to John's Vectra and got in that.

Back at John's we counted out the money. We'd got away with £60,000. That was twenty thousand each because only three of us did the job. After we put the money away we burned our clothes and the plates.

The weekend came and we were all going out to town to celebrate. Katie and I got into Scottie's BM and we drove to the pub to meet up with John. We hit town at about ten. First we went to Bar Med, then to 21's. We walked up to the doors, shook the bouncers' hands and went in. We didn't have to pay anywhere now. After 21's we went to the Dolby Hotel. At reception we booked in the master suite. There were me and Katie, with John, Scottie, Andy and their birds, so we needed a few rooms.

The party was going with a swing. We got room service to bring us up food and drink. Katie and the other girls had gone down to the bar to meet another mate and bring her up to join us. So it was just us lads when the door was suddenly booted in.

"Armed police! Nobody move!"

I felt ill when I heard them. Then I panicked.

I saw Scottie run to the window. He opened it and jumped out. I went to do the same. I was about to leap. An arm came round my neck. Someone dragged me to the floor.

"Where do you think you're going, sunshine?"

"Fuck you!"

"You're the one who's fucked, son."

Before he clicked the bracelets on me I had time for one thought. At least Katie's out of this. She would have the sense to go home to her Mum's. I just hoped she wouldn't see me being taken down to the van.

Chapter Ten

"Your solicitor's here," the copper said.

I was taken from my cell to an interview room.

"What the fuck's going on?" I asked my solicitor.

"I don't know yet. They won't tell me anything.

"Is Scottie here with us?"

"No. They've not got him."

That nearly brought a smile to my face. I'd seen him jump through the window, but I didn't know if he'd been caught or not. My solicitor told me that I was being held until the warrant for a search of my house came through. That was all they'd told him for the time being.

I was led back to my cell.

Once I was there all sorts of questions were going round my head. How did they know we were in that hotel? Was it the guy whose head I whacked? They knew something serious – they don't send armed response out for something stupid.

I'd been in the police station for four days when my solicitor came back to tell me what was going on.

"So when am I getting bail?" I asked. I was pissed off.

"I'm afraid it's unlikely you'll get bail. They've got you on three armed robberies and four other robberies. And they found £10,000 in a cash tin under your bed. All your clothes have been taken for forensic. And your car's been impounded."

"How long am I looking at?"

"Hard to say. It depends on the evidence."

"What about John and Andy? What's going on with them?"

"Same thing as you. You're all in court tomorrow."

"To get remanded?" I asked.

"More than likely."

Within five minutes of being up in court the next morning we were all remanded in custody.

Epilogue

At Manchester Crown Court in March 2004:

John was sentenced to 14 years in prison.

Andy was sentenced to 10 years in prison.

Matt was sentenced to 15 years in prison.

After being on the run for a few months, Jim Scott was caught and received a 15-year sentence for his part in the robberies.

After he was sentenced, Matt broke up with Katie because he didn't want her to wait that long for him.

Glossary

agg-twoc	the charge for getting chased in a car and getting nicked
assoc	association – leisure time on your wing in prison
balis	balaclavas
blagged	told lies
capped	taking the cap off the back of a car's ignition
ching	cocaine
dibble	police
dimp	cigarette stub
graft	to do a crime for money
grid	iron drain cover
hotters	getting chased by the police
mazies	nickname for maisonettes
mix	cigarette tobacco and cannabis together
Mocha Parade	a parade of shops in Salford
old-skool	dance music from the early 1990s
Oscar's	a clothes shop in Manchester which sells designer and sports clothes
pins	part of the steering lock mechanism
prison number	your ID in prison. The number lasts for your whole sentence
rams	ram raids – using a car to smash through a window and rob a shop
scanner	a radio tuned to police frequencies
sweat box	the van that takes you from court to prison
toasting	burning cigarettes to make them dry for a mix
weed	cannabis